To Kathryn Cole,
who keeps the sky from falling.

Henny Penny

H. Werner Zimmermann

SCHOLASTIC INC.

New York   Toronto   London   Auckland   Sydney

ISBN 0-590-42389-4

Text copyright © 1989 by Scholastic-TAB Publications Ltd.
Illustrations copyright © 1989 by H. Werner Zimmermann.

All rights reserved. Published by Scholastic Inc.,
730 Broadway, New York, NY 10003, by arrangement with
Scholastic-TAB Publications Ltd., Canada.

49 48 47 46 45 44   14/0

Printed in the U.S.A.   40

One day Henny Penny
was eating corn in the farmyard
when . . .

whack! . . . an acorn fell on her head.

"Oh, my," said Henny Penny.
"The sky is falling! The sky is falling.
I must go and tell the King."

So she went along and she went along and she went along until she met Cocky Locky.

"Hello, Henny Penny," said Cocky Locky.
"Where are you going?"

"The sky is falling and I must go
and tell the King," said Henny Penny.

"Oh! May I go with you?" asked Cocky Locky.

"Certainly!" said Henny Penny.

So they went along and they went along and they went along until they met Ducky Lucky.

"Hello, Henny Penny and Cocky Locky,"
said Ducky Lucky. "Where are you going?"

"The sky is falling and
we must go and tell the King,"
said Henny Penny and Cocky Locky.

"Oh! May I go with you?"
asked Ducky Lucky.

"Certainly!" said Henny Penny
and Cocky Locky.

So they went along and they went along and they went along until they met Goosey Loosey.

"Hello, Henny Penny, Cocky Locky and Ducky Lucky," said Goosey Loosey. "Where are you going?"

"The sky is falling and we must go and tell the King," said Henny Penny, Cocky Locky and Ducky Lucky.

"Oh! May I go with you?" asked Goosey Loosey.

"Certainly!" said Henny Penny, Cocky Locky and Ducky Lucky.

So they went along and they went along and
they went along until they met Turkey Lurkey.

"Hello, Henny Penny, Cocky Locky, Ducky Lucky and Goosey Loosey," said Turkey Lurkey. "Where are you going?"

"The sky is falling and we must go and tell
the King," said Henny Penny, Cocky Locky,
Ducky Lucky and Goosey Loosey.

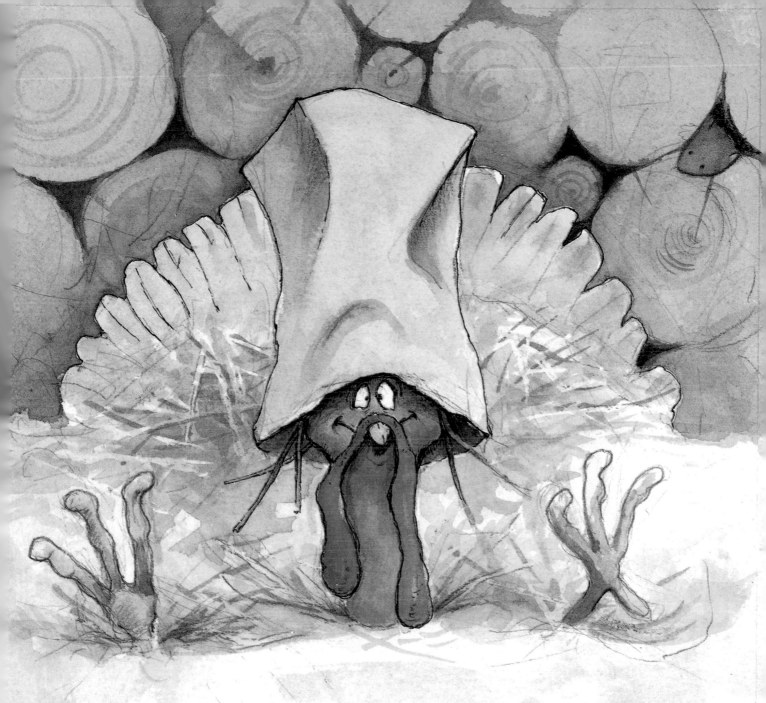

"Oh! May I go with you?" asked Turkey Lurkey.

"Certainly!" said Henny Penny, Cocky Locky,
Ducky Lucky and Goosey Loosey.

So they went along and they went along

and they went along until they met Foxy Loxy.

"Greetings, Henny Penny, Cocky Locky,
Ducky Lucky, Goosey Loosey and
Turkey Lurkey," said Foxy Loxy.
"Where are you going?"

"The sky is falling and we must go and tell
the King," said Henny Penny, Cocky Locky,
Ducky Lucky, Goosey Loosey and
Turkey Lurkey.

"You'll never get there in time," said Foxy Loxy. "Come with me and I'll show you the shortcut."

"Certainly!" said Henny Penny,
Cocky Locky, Ducky Lucky,
Goosey Loosey and Turkey Lurkey.
And they followed Foxy Loxy
right into his cave.

Henny Penny, Cocky Locky, Ducky Lucky, Goosey Loosey and Turkey Lurkey were never seen again . . .

. . . and no one ever told the King
the sky was falling.